The story of a little mouse trapped in a book

STORY AND PICTURES
BY MONIQUE FELIX

1980 by Editions Tournesol-Carabosse S.A.
1025, Saint-Sulpice Switzerland

Copyright © 1981 by Moonlight Publishing Ltd
for the English edition.

Printed in Italy by La Editoriale Libraria.

methuen moonlight

ISBN 0 907144 28 4